Friends of DENSA:

CONGRATULATIONS on your decision to take THE DENSA QUIZ! Now you'll find out just how DENSE you really are!

But, you're lucky. It wasn't always this easy to discover your denseness. There was a time when thousands of dense people went through life branded as misfits and under-achievers. They were at the mercy of the quick wits and impossible questions of snooty intellectuals, personnel managers, computer brains. No one would even *dare* to be dense in the privacy of their own homes. There was no way to find out your D.Q. (Density Quotient). Dense people would even avoid each other in the street. It was terrible.

Finally, a few of us decided: "Pooh-Pooh on I.Q.—We'd rather be Dense!" and The International DENSA Society was born. It started out as a place where dense men and women could meet, exchange dense experiences, and just get dense together. It has since grown into the densest society in the world today, thanks to you and the over-whelming popularity of THE DENSA QUIZ.

Now, don't be nervous about taking THE QUIZ. Chances are you're denser than you think. Just sit back, relax, take out your No.

2 crayon and answer as many questions as you want. Whenever you're not sure just guess, or write your own answer if you think it's denser than the one listed. *Every answer has a potential D.Q.* All instructions and guidelines are just suggestions so you don't have to follow them strictly. You can even make up your own questions. The idea is to get as dense as you can.

When you're finished, send your answers* along with any questions* you've come up with and a large stamped, self-addressed envelope to:

D.Q.
The International DENSA Society
P.O. Box 214338
Dallas, TX 75221

Our staff at DENSA will go through all the material that you send in and get back to you about your Density Quotient. You'll also receive what we call a DENSE-PAK of all sorts of goodies, courtesy of DENSA.

Good luck and Stay Dense!

Stephen Price
President

*Note: It is understood that any material relating to THE DENSA QUIZ sent to either Avon Books or The International DENSA Society shall become the sole property of Avon Books and The International DENSA Society, who shall each have the right to use or license of the material with or without your name in any future publications.

THE
DENSA QUIZ

—THE—
DENSA QUIZ

THE OFFICIAL AND COMPLETE D.Q. TEST OF THE INTERNATIONAL DENSA SOCIETY

COMPILED BY STEPHEN PRICE

FOUNDER OF THE INTERNATIONAL DENSA SOCIETY

Illustrations by Christopher L. Dinas

AVON
PUBLISHERS OF BARD, CAMELOT, DISCUS AND FLARE BOOKS

AVON BOOKS
A division of
The Hearst Corporation
1790 Broadway
New York, New York 10019

First Avon Printing, December, 1983

Acknowledgments

The first person I must thank is Brian Sumrall for following the path to Dorothy's laugh. Heartfelt thanks to my dense editor, Paul Dinas, who bought me a raincoat when I needed it most, my agent Knox Burger, who'd probably rather be fishing, Mark Kessel for his "veg-control," and Liz for her unwavering faith.

Special thanks to my friends for their support: Norman & Janie, Dr. Jeffrey Sandler, Griff Atticus, Steve & Nancy, Gena & Quacky, Joe Willy's, Mindy & Carl, Larry Postel, Joe Libs, Bob Werber, Mike Russ, Mike Marz & Mike Peterson, Judy, Bill, Matt, Gretchen, Ritchie Angelo, Dr. Sharpe, Mom, Dad & Carlos!

And to Lani and Molly who gave me Chinese food and love!

THE
DENSA QUIZ

1. Life as we know it exists on this planet because of junk food, nuclear waste and Hollywood.

   a. True

   b. False

   c. Which planet?

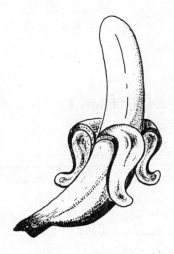

2. What do four out of five people think of FIRST when you mention the word BANANA? Explain.

DENSA Word Crunch

3. Find the five names in this crunch.

MCCARTNEYLENNONBEATLESSTARRHARRISON

4. Define UNIVERSE. Give two examples.

a. _____

_____

b. _____

_____

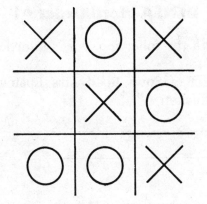

5. Whose turn is it?

    a. X

    b. O

    c. Neither X nor O

    d. Impossible to tell from illustration

6. Name three American cities that DON'T have restaurants with golden arches.

_____

_____

_____

DENSA Word Order #1

7. Put the following words in order:

a. Egg, Soup, Road, Mrs. Epstein, Chicken

———————, ———————, ———————,

———————, ———————

b. Intercourse, Cigarette, Headache, Foreplay, Polaroid

———————, ———————, ———————,

———————, ———————

8. How many bags should you bring on an ego trip?

9. It is a scientific fact that people who eat food will live longer than people who do not eat food.

a. True

b. False

c. Other

10. The Optimists Club is having their annual recruitment meeting tonight. Old members are scheduled to arrive at 7:00 p.m. and prospective new members at 8:00 p.m.

Do the Optimists become pessimists wondering whether or not any new members will show up? Explain.

_____

_____

_____

_____

11. Find the misspelled word:
   a. Ocean
   b. Government
   c. Tissue
   d. Fig
   e. Pencil
   f. Non of the above

12. Lay out six nickels and six pennies on a table as shown below. Using any combination of coins, make the total value equal 36¢.

13. "Avogadros Number" is a scientific formula for:

a. Guacamole dip

b. Calling Avogadros

c. Determining how many fish are in the oceans of the world

d. Some of the above

e. Other

14. The term LOVE is the Anglicized version of the French word L'OEUF, which means egg. L'OEUF is French slang for ZERO because the symbol 0 looks like an egg.

Therefore, LOVE may be said to be roughly equivalent to:

a. A western omelette

b. Nothing

c. A 99¢ Breakfast Special

d. Unsure

15. The geography of a region will have the GREATEST influence on its inhabitants':

a. Plumbing

b. Body gestures

c. Bathroom reading

16. Which of the following is a nonelectrolyte:

a. HNO_3

b. HCl

c. Candles

d. CBS TV

e. $Ba(OH)_2$

17. How many stars are in the sky?

    a. All of the above

DENSA Complete the Cliché

18. "Love is a many splendored

    _____."

19. Elvis Presley was better known as
_____.

20. Pimentos may best be described as:

a. Jewelry worn on women's heads in India

b. Toes of the pimen bird

c. Small dark animals that clung to Bogie's body in the film "The African Queen"

d. None of the above

e. Other

21. DENSA Word Puzzle

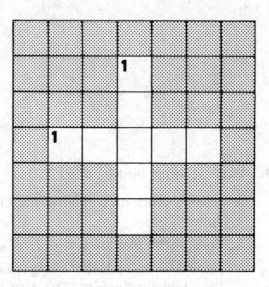

ACROSS

1. Plural of HEAD

DOWN

1. Two _____ are better than one.

22. When you get out of the surf on a dry summer day, you feel cool because:

    a. You are dripping wet

    b. The ocean is salty

    c. You have a perfect tan

23. Which word does NOT rhyme with the others?

    a. Bar

    b. Car

    c. Miscellaneous

    d. Jar

    e. Star

24. How far is it from HERE to THERE? Show work below.

25. A LASER is NOT:

  a. Future means of interstellar travel

  b. Someone who sits around and watches TV all day

  c. A ladies' blazer

  d. A kind of kitchen utensil

  e. Two of the above

26. A child is injured in an accident and rushed to the hospital. Doctor Anna Hildergarde takes one look at the child and says: "I can't treat this boy, he's my son." The doctor is NOT the child's father.

In the space below, explain Dr. Hildergarde's reaction. Be specific.

_____

_____

_____

_____

27. Driving on a very hot road, you may sometimes see what appears to be a large body of water instead of the surface of the approaching road. The reason for this is:

a. Submarine currents

b. Hydrogen peroxide

c. Abuse of controlled substances

d. Other

28. What figure comes next in the series?

    a. ♠

    b. ♡

    c. ♣

    d. ◇

29. If some Bifurs are Bofurs and all Gloins are Bofurs, then some Bifurs are definitely Gloins.

    a. True

    b. Ridiculous because of inbreeding

    c. False

    d. Matter of opinion

30. Divide the pie into eight pieces by making ONLY eight cuts. Each piece need NOT be equal in size.

31. If the French philosopher is right and there is NO EXIT, then how would he explain all those little red signs in movie theaters? Footnote where appropriate.

32. The OPPOSITE of HUNGRY is:

    a. Thirsty

    b. Tired

    c. Polish

    d. Not hungry

33. I'm OK, You're OK.

    a. True

    b. False

    c. Other

34. Under international law, if a plane crashes in the middle of Canada, where would the plane be buried?

35. An example of instinctual behavior in man is:

   a. Arm wrestling

   b. Sleeping

   c. Drinking beer

   d. Heavy petting

   e. All of the above

DENSA Word Order #2

36. Put the following words in alphabetical order:

ABLE	_____
BEATNIK	_____
CEILING	_____
DELIGHT	_____
EDICT	_____
FUDGE	_____
GARGLE	_____
HUMBLE	_____
IDIOT	_____
JAZZ	_____
KETCHUP	_____
LUNAR	_____
MOUSE	_____
NUCLEAR	_____
ONLY	_____
PEACE	_____
QUIT	_____
RUSTIC	_____
STINK	_____
TUB	_____
UNDERCUT	_____
VIVACIOUS	_____
WINK	_____
XMAS	_____
YAK	_____
ZOO	_____

37. Of the twenty stores on Main Street, two have neon lights and 18 have awnings. One could conclude that:

a. Not many people will get wet walking on the street in the rain

b. Awnings are cheaper than neon

c. A few people will get wet walking on the street in the rain

d. Other

38. A NOMAD is:

a. A person that is NOT mad

b. The predecessor of beatnik

c. A top secret government agency

d. Space advertisement in a Nome newspaper

e. Other

39. Which triangle is larger?

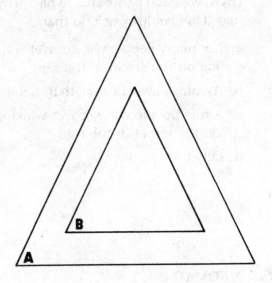

40. Which one of the five is LEAST like the other four?

   a. Five
   b. Other four
   c. Other four
   d. Other four
   e. Other four

DENSA Sentence Sense

41. Punctuate this sentence correctly:

I yam wot I yam and dats all dat I yam

42. Bob usually beats Cindy at tennis, but loses to Tom. Jim is busy at work. Carl wins most of the time against Cindy, and sometimes against Bob, but cannot beat Tom.

Who doesn't play tennis at all?

_____

43. Who doesn't fit in?

a. George Washington

b. Liberace

c. Abraham Lincoln

d. John Adams

DENSA Quote Question

44. Match the saying with the sayer.

_____ To be or not to be
_____ Do Bee or Don't Bee
_____ Do be do be do
_____ To do is to be

a. Frank Sinatra

b. Jean-Paul Sartre

c. Alexander Hamilton

d. Miss Mary Ann

e. Porky Pig

f. Hamlet

45. In one, two or three sentences, explain why the previous page is blank.

_____

_____

_____

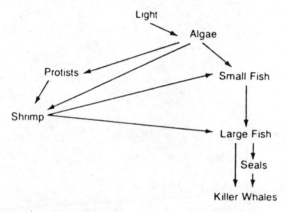

46. What conclusion can be drawn from the diagram?

a. Killer whales disappear at night

b. Protists prefer algae to shrimp

c. Nothing about the French Revolution

d. Other

47. BISECT is:

    a. A couple of insects

    b. The gay district of a city

    c. A liqueur

    d. Unsure

48. Which of the following is NOT a status symbol:

    a. A new Mercedes

    b. Beets

    c. A son who's a doctor

    d. An oil well

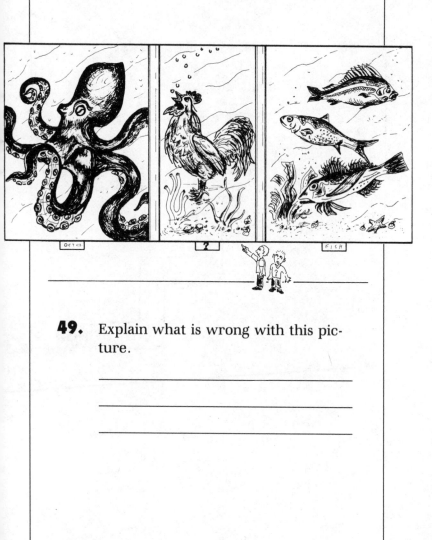

49. Explain what is wrong with this picture.

_____

_____

_____

50. **DENSA Maze Test**

Time Limit: 20 minutes

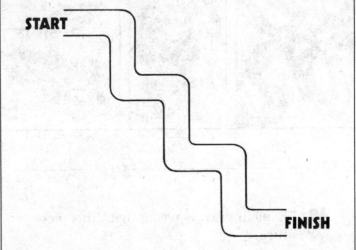

START

FINISH

51. What shape is an ice cube when wet?

52. Five sailors raced their boats off the Florida coast. There were no ties. Bob didn't come in first. John was neither first nor last. Joe came in one place after Bob. James was NOT second. Walt was two places behind James.

Which sailor did NOT finish the race? Explain.

53. Gossip travels FASTEST through:

    a. First class postage

    b. Water

    c. The grapevine

    d. Drums

    e. Other

54. The theory that living things may spring from nonliving matter is BEST described as:

    a. Magic

    b. Immaculate Conception

    c. Spontaneous combustion

    d. Silly

55. How long does it take the average person to run the gamut?

56. SYNECDOCHE and METONYMY are:

a. Characters in a Shakespearean tragedy

b. Irrelevant

c. S & M

d. A famous burlesque act

57. BUOY is:

   a. A rock singer
   b. A kind of knife
   c. Not a girl
   d. Unsure

58. How much dirt is there in a hole six feet wide, twelve feet deep and thirty feet long? Round off answer to the nearest ton.

DENSA Inkblot Test #1

59. What shape does this suggest?

60. What figure does this suggest?

DENSA Inkblot Test #3

61. What scene does this suggest?

62. Locate as many states of conscious-
ness as you can on the map below.

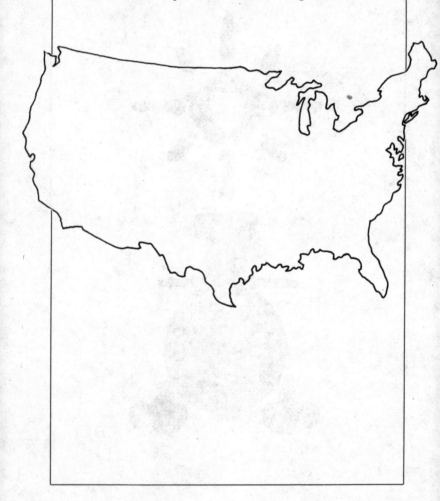

63. SYMPATHY is:

   a. Another name for orchestra

   b. No desire, lack of interest

   c. Something you get when you don't want it

   d. Other

64. Newton's three laws explain:

   a. Driving without a license

   b. Proper use of a waterbed

   c. Motion sickness

   d. All of the above

65. Using one and only one unbroken horizontal line, bisect the above six vertical lines.

66. Which does NOT belong with the others:

   a. Dada

   b. Abstract Realism

   c. Cubism

   d. Mama

DENSA Trick Questions

67. Fill in the correct question to correspond to the answers below. No time limit.

a. A hummingbird's wings.

_____

b. On the pads of his paws.

_____

c. From an airplane, with the plane's window directly in the center.

_____

d. Clark Kent.

_____

68. The majority of the world's water supply is in bottles.

a. True

b. False

DENSA Food Shape Test

69. Match the food with its corresponding shape as pictured below.

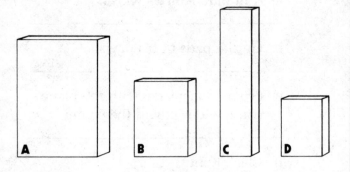

____ Rice
____ Corn flakes
____ Prunes
____ Spaghetti

70. Which of the following substances is MOST important to all cell activity?

a. Bread

b. Water

c. Protoplasm

d. Hard drugs

e. None of the above

71. Attempts have been made to improve the genetic makeup of the human race by:

a. Changing cosmetic companies

b. Building more parks

c. Inventing better sun lamps

d. All of the above

72. Napoleon Bonaparte was defeated at the Battle of Waterloo because:

a. The French supply lines were exhausted

b. It was a particularly harsh winter

c. The British had a superior military strategy

d. He forgot to trim the nails on his right hand before the battle

DENSA Food Group Test

73. Match the food group with the corresponding food as pictured below.
(Hint: There may be more than one answer for each group.)

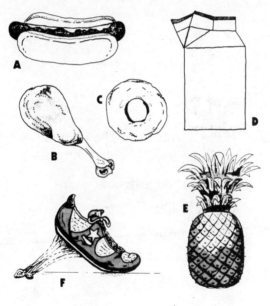

_____ Meat
_____ Dessert
_____ Dairy
_____ Fruit
_____ Gum on shoe

74. DENSA Complete the Cliché

"Give me liberty or give me
_____."

75. If the cerebellum of a pigeon were destroyed, it would NOT be able to:

a. Avoid pedestrians

b. Walk like a pigeon

c. Reproduce

d. Ruin park statues

e. Other

76. RIGMAROLE is:

a. Greek pastry

b. Prevalent in religious circles

c. The central character in an Italian opera

d. Yacht hardware

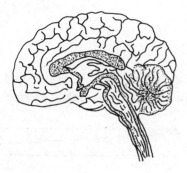

77. This is an illustration of:

a. The city of New Orleans

b. An embryo

c. The inside of a lollypop

d. All of the above

78. Probably the most likely reason why dinosaurs became extinct was that they:

    a. Took up too much space

    b. Refused to change with the times

    c. Look great in museums

    d. Refused to wear designer jeans

    e. Unsure

79. Who, What, When, Where, Why and How? Give an example of each.

_____

_____

_____

_____

_____

_____

80.   **DENSA Sentence Sense**

Fix this sentence:
He put the horse before the cart.

81. DKSLSKD LDKDKDODOJ DK DSBAEIECNKD?

a. UEKDNLANCIEL IDL ISIDLY

b. LDK KSOSOD

c. KFIED CIDIDLS

d. None of the above

82. In what year would you expect to have the HIGHEST umbrella sales?

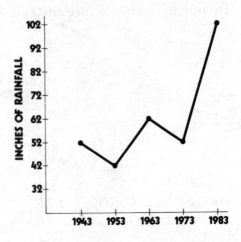

a. 1943

b. 1953

c. 1963

d. 1973

e. 1983

83. Polly Ester Sutes was a 19th Century spinster known for her poor taste in fashion.

a. True

b. False

84. Can you find the needle in the hay stack?

Time limit: 15 minutes